A book
is a present you can open
again and again.

THIS BOOK BELONGS TO

Mayra Lara

FROM

Mayra Lara

The Elves & the Shoemaker

Adapted from a German fairy tale by the Brothers Grimm

General Editor
Bernice E. Cullinan
New York University

Retold by
Seva Spanos

Illustrated by
Yoshi Miyake

TREASURE TREE ™

World Book, Inc.
a Scott Fetzer company
Chicago   London   Sydney   Toronto

$\mathcal{L}$ong, long ago, in a little cottage near a small village, there lived a shoemaker and his wife. They had grown old and slow, and their chores left them more and more tired with each passing day. Yet even though they worked hard from morning till night, they were very poor.

In fact, the old couple grew poorer and poorer until, one cold November day, there wasn't a bit of food left to eat in their cottage. Things were so bad even the mice had moved away.

What was worse, the shoemaker had only enough leather to make one more pair of shoes. "I hope these turn out well," he said. "If we don't sell them, we'll have no food for the winter ahead." The old couple worried and worried, with just the wind to keep them company in their drafty old cottage.

hen the wife found a small bit of flour and sugar. This cheered the good lady. "I know," she said. "I'll make a batch of sweet cookies to sell at the market tomorrow!" Then she frowned. "But we'll have to build a strong fire to bake them."

"Since you're doing the cooking, I'll build the fire," her husband replied. So he put on his tattered old coat and went out into the freezing night to get some wood.

nce outside, the shoemaker spotted a large log that he could split into smaller pieces. But just as he started to heave his heavy ax, he noticed a wooden box nearby. Inside was a tidy heap of twigs and leaves.

"I wonder where this box came from," the shoemaker thought. "It is very old, and the twigs and leaves will make good kindling. We'll burn this box." And burn it, they did.

That evening, the warmth of the fire and the smell of sweet cookies filled the cottage. But there was no dinner to eat. Hungry and tired, the shoemaker cut the leather for the shoes. Setting it aside on his workbench, he said, "Morning will come soon enough. I'll finish the shoes then."

The shoemaker's wife had made enough dough for a dozen cookies, with one left over—13 in all. The old couple were very hungry, but they split just the extra cookie to share—one-half for each. They had to save all the rest to sell.

When not a crumb was left, the shoemaker thanked his wife for the delicious treat. "We'll have no trouble selling these cookies tomorrow," he said. "But we've both worked hard today. Now it is time for us to rest."

Filled with hope, the two said their prayers. Then they fluffed their pillows, climbed into bed, and pulled up their covers. Soon they were fast asleep, dreaming of a time when they could hear children whispering in the night, and feel a little boy and girl scrambling up the bedcovers to be near them.

The morning brought a big surprise. When the husband set to work, he found the pair of shoes on his workbench completely finished. Every stitch was perfectly sewn. Some big leather scraps were in a neat pile, but there were no little scraps to be seen. The workbench was as tidy as could be. The shoemaker did not know what to think.

He was surprised again to hear a cry from his wife. "One of the cookies is gone!" she wailed. "We needed an even dozen to sell. What could have happened to it!"

The couple looked closely where the cookie had been. All that was left was a trail of tiny crumbs that led off the table, onto a chair, down to the floor, and across the room to the mousehole. And there it stopped.

"The mice must be back," the wife concluded. "Perhaps the warm fire and food attracted them."

But there was a final surprise that morning—the biggest surprise of all. At the mousehole, the couple discovered a tiny doormat made of a leather scrap. And on two shiny shoe nails hung two tattered little caps.

"These are a new kind of mice," the shoemaker said.

Suddenly a customer clomped through the door. The new shoes fit him perfectly! In fact, they were so handsome and well-made that the customer insisted on paying even more than the couple asked. With the money from selling the shoes, they were able to buy enough leather for two more pairs.

That evening, the shoemaker cut out this leather, and his wife made more cookies. By morning, another cookie had vanished, but two pairs of new shoes had appeared! The shoemaker cut leather for four pairs the next day, then eight, then sixteen—twice as many pairs of shoes each day in exchange for one cookie each night!

oon the shoemaker could no longer keep up with his helpers. As news of the fine work spread, wealthy families began to invite him to their homes so that they could try on his shoes. Very often, they would buy everything he had brought with him and then order even more. Each night, the shoemaker cut out as much leather as he could. And his mysterious helpers always had the shoes completely finished by morning.

One day just before Christmas, something new appeared in the cottage. Instead of tattered caps, wee leather hats hung on the nails at the mousehole. Now the shoemaker and his wife became so curious that they decided to find out who their helpers were. So they left a candle burning that night and hid behind a curtain, waiting to see what would happen.

t the stroke of midnight, a tiny little elf man and his tiny little wife crept out of the mousehole, scurried up a chair, and leapt onto the workbench. Except for their new leather hats, their clothes were all in rags. They began to stitch and hammer so cleverly and so quickly that the couple could barely follow. The elves didn't stop until all the shoes were finished. Then they grabbed some small leather scraps and disappeared into the mousehole, taking a cookie with them.

The next morning, the shoemaker's wife said, "Those little people have helped us so much. We'll never be poor and hungry again, but they have nothing to cover them in this drafty house except old rags. They need our help.

"So for Christmas, I'll make them a dress, a suit, coats and scarves, and some warm socks. And you make each of them a tiny pair of gloves and a tiny pair of boots." The thought delighted the shoemaker, so he and his wife set to work.

By Christmas Eve, the outfits were finished. Instead of the cut-out work, the couple placed their gifts on the workbench. As a treat, the wife left special Christmas cookies with creamy icing. Then the couple hid behind the curtain again.

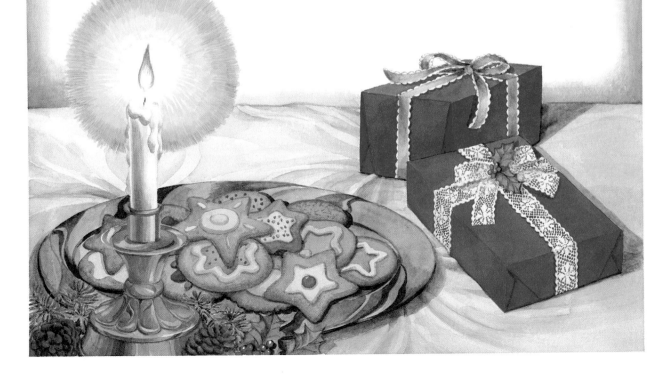

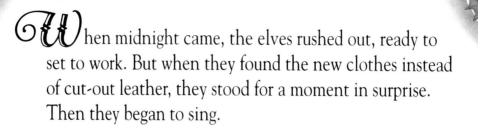

When midnight came, the elves rushed out, ready to set to work. But when they found the new clothes instead of cut-out leather, they stood for a moment in surprise. Then they began to sing.

Oh, look inside this pretty box!
A little dress, some little socks!
Do you suppose they're meant for me?
I'm sure they can't be meant for me.
No, they were never meant for me.

Look! Over here, I see a suit,
Two pairs of gloves, two pairs of boots.
Do you suppose they're gifts for us?
I'm sure they can't be gifts for us.
No, they were never gifts for us.

These clothes are fair! These clothes are fine!
But those aren't yours, and these aren't mine.
Now, how will we keep warm tonight
Without a stitch of work in sight?
There's not a stitch of work in sight!

Imagine what they'd think of these
Beyond the town, beyond the trees
Where elves are trimming wreath and bough
And tree for Christmas right about now.
Home looks so pretty right about now.

With snowflakes flying all around
And snowdrifts growing mound by mound,
Do you suppose we'd make it there
In clothes like these? We'd make it there.
I know that we could make it there!

These clothes are gifts—it must be true.
One-half's for me, one-half's for you!
These clothes are fair! These clothes are fine!
These clothes mean home at Christmastime!
Come on, let's go! It's Christmastime!

The elves dashed into the mousehole with their gifts and soon came out bundled up in their new clothes. Each carried a tiny leather patchwork bag filled with bits of cookies. After one final look around the cottage, they danced out the door into the night.

The shoemaker and his wife never saw the elves again. But they always cherished these reminders that the elves had left behind: two tattered caps, a tiny leather doormat, and a special Christmas cookie, on which the elves had written Love.

To Parents

Children delight in hearing and reading fairy tales. *The Elves & the Shoemaker* will provide your child with an entertaining story as well as a bridge into learning some important concepts. Here are a few easy and natural ways your child can express feelings and understandings about the story. You know your child and can best judge which ideas will be the most enjoyable.

The elves got into the shoemaker's house in an unusual way. Look through the story with your child to find the picture that shows how. Enjoy guessing some ways these little people could get into your house — in a grocery bag, a purse, or even in someone's pocket, for example.

The elves in the story are as helpful as can be. When you and your child visit businesses or offices in your community, point out the different workers. Ask, "What do people do here? Do you think they would like the elves to help them? How could the elves help?"

Pick any page in the story and reread each sentence. Help your child find things in the picture that go with words your child may not know. For example, in the first picture, find and talk about the cottage, the shoemaker, the wife, and chores. Share each page this way to help your child build an understanding of any unfamiliar words.

The elves secretly helped the shoemaker and his wife. Help your child find ways to secretly do nice things for people in your family. Enjoy discussing the results, but try to keep the helper's identity a secret!

Help your child cut out old magazine pictures that show daytime and nighttime scenes. Paste the pictures into booklets with the titles "Sunshine" and "Moonglow." Talk about what the story's characters do during the day and night. Ask your child to draw some pictures of what the characters do and add the pictures to your booklets.

The elves were good at doubling shoes. Practice doubling at your house with elbow macaroni or puffed cereal. Start with one piece. Add another piece to get two. Double that to get four. Keep going until you get to any big number. Remember to help your child count as you double the amounts.